lunch

This book is for Rochelle

Special thanks to Laura for her patience and
to David and Indigo for their endurance

Henry Holt and Company
Publishers since 1866
175 Fifth Avenue, New York, NY 10010
mackids.com

Henry Holt® is a registered trademark of
Macmillan Publishing Group, LLC.

Library of Congress Cataloging-in-Publication Data
Fleming, Denise.
Lunch / written and illustrated by Denise Fleming.
Summary: A very hungry mouse eats a large lunch
comprised of colorful foods.
[1. Mice—Fiction. 2. Food habits—Fiction. 3. Color—Fiction.]
I. Title. PZ7.F5994Lu 1993 [E]—dc20 92-178

First published in hardcover in 1992 by Henry Holt and Company
First paperback edition—1995
Printed in China by RR Donnelley Asia Printing Solutions Ltd.,
Dongguan City, Guangdong Province

ISBN 978-0-8050-1636-9 (hardcover)
20 19 18 17 16

ISBN 978-1-250-23228-1 (2018 hardcover)
10 9 8 7 6 5 4 3 2 1

ISBN 978-0-8050-4646-5 (paperback)
35 34

The illustrations were created in handmade paper.

lunch
Denise Fleming

SQUARE FISH • Henry Holt and Company • New York

Mouse was *very* hungry.
He was so hungry,

he ate
a crisp
white —

turnip,

tasty

orange —

carrots,

sweet
yellow —

corn,

tender
green —

peas,

tart
blue —

berries,

sour

purple —

grapes,

shiny
red —

apples,

and juicy pink —

watermelon,

crunchy
black seeds
and all.

Then,

he took a nap
until . . .